# Gathering Sparks

Howard Schwartz

Illustrated by Kristina Swarner

Roaring Brook Press  New York

Once, when you were little,
your grandfather came to visit.
That night the moon was full and
the sky was filled with stars.
Your grandfather said,
"The sky's so clear tonight. Let's go outside."

So you went out into the yard, where fireflies
lit up the dark and crickets chirped with all
their might. You and your grandfather
peered up at the sky, crowded with stars.
For a long time no one spoke, and then you asked,

"Where did all the stars come from?"

And your grandfather said,
"Long, long ago, before this world
was created, God sent forth
ten vessels, like a fleet of ships, each
carrying its cargo of light.

If those vessels had reached their destination,
the world would have been perfect.
But the further they traveled,
the more fragile they became.

Finally the vessels shattered,
scattering sparks of light
throughout the heavens.
And that is how the stars
came into being.

And you said, "Oh."
And you looked up at the sky
filled with glowing sparks,
and you saw the stars as if
for the first time.

Then your grandfather said,
"But the sparks did not only fall in heaven,
they fell everywhere, in so many places
that God needed our help to gather them.
That's why we were created—
to gather the sparks, to gather the sparks
no matter where they are hidden."

And you asked,

"But how can sparks be gathered?"

And your grandfather said,
"Every time you do a good deed,
one of the sparks is set free.
When you plant a tree,
a spark rises up.

When you help your baby sister,
a spark can be seen in her eyes.

And when you are kind to animals, a spark of kindness enters the world."

"For every good deed you do,
one of those hidden sparks rises up
and a little bit of the world is repaired.
And one day, when enough of those sparks
have been gathered, the broken vessels will be
restored, and there will be peace in the world."

Then your grandfather picked you up, gently,
and carried you inside. And as he was
carrying you, he whispered,
"And most of all, sparks are
gathered whenever you
love someone."

And then he hugged you so tight, you closed your eyes.

And when you opened them, you saw sparks glowing everywhere.

For Ari and Ava —H.S.   ✳   For Sam and Sara —K.S.

## About This Book

One of the most important and beloved concepts of Jewish tradition is what is known as *tikkun olam* or repair of the world. This concept proposes that everyone should do their part in trying to improve the world by becoming environmentally aware, by seeking peace, and by living one's life with the awareness of the needs of others. A good case can be made that *tikkun olam* has inspired the environmental movement that has played a central role throughout the world in this century.

The concept of *tikkun olam* comes from the teachings of Rabbi Isaac Luria who lived in the city of Safed in northern Israel in the sixteenth century. The myth of the shattering of the vessels and gathering of the sparks told in this story was the central teaching of the Ari, as Rabbi Luria was known.

Coming, as it did, a century after the expulsion of the Jews from Spain in 1492, this myth provided an explanation for God permitting the Jews of Spain to be scattered throughout the world. Instead of seeing their exile in far-flung countries as a punishment, the myth explained that God had put them in those places for a purpose—to gather the sparks. This gathering took place whenever a person performed good deeds, which, the myth explained, had the effect of repairing the world. Eventually the world would be restored to its pristine condition. In this way the Ari turned the punishment of the expulsion from Spain into a blessing.

In any case, the myth of the Ari is exceptionally beautiful and explains that every person has a role to play in the destiny of the world. It reminds us that everything we do has consequences, and that God is counting on us to maintain our beautiful world.

Text copyright 2010 by Howard Schwartz ✳ Illustrations copyright 2010 by Kristina Swarner
Published by Roaring Brook Press
Roaring Brook Press is a division of Holtzbrinck Publishing Holdings Limited Partnership, 175 Fifth Avenue, New York, New York 10010 ✳ www.roaringbrookpress.com
All rights reserved
Distributed in Canada by H. B. Fenn and Company Ltd.
Library of Congress Cataloging-in-Publication Data
Schwartz, Howard, 1945-
  Gathering sparks / Howard Schwartz ; illustrated by Kristina Swarner. —1st ed.
    p. cm.
  Summary: A grandfather introduces his grandson to the Jewish tradition of tikkun olam, a centuries-old concept which proposes that everyone must do their part in order to improve the world.
  ISBN 978-1-59643-280-2
  1. Jewish way of life—Fiction. 2. Conduct of life—Fiction. 3. Grandfathers—Fiction.   I. Swarner, Kristina, ill. II. Title.
  PZ7.S4078Gat 2010
  [E]—dc22
                          2009042238

Roaring Brook Press books are available for special promotions and premiums. For details contact: Director of Special Markets, Holtzbrinck Publishers.
First Edition  August 2010
Book design by CoolKidsGraphics Inc,
Printed in April 2010 in China by South China Printing Co. Ltd., Dongguan City, Guangdong Province
10 9 8 7 6 5 4 3 2 1